Snozz

Gargoyle

Snorky

Gumph

Jarred

crab

Nessie

Matilda

Eyeball

Sloppy

Trog

Hairy

Slither

Hag

Bull

Snout

Rough

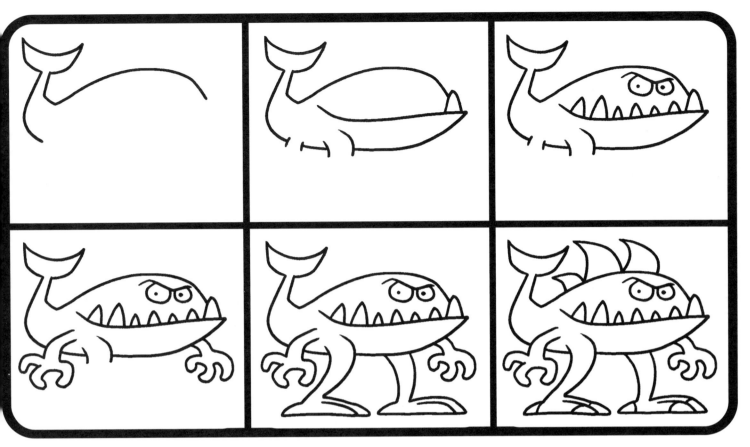

Troll-In-The-Box

Batty

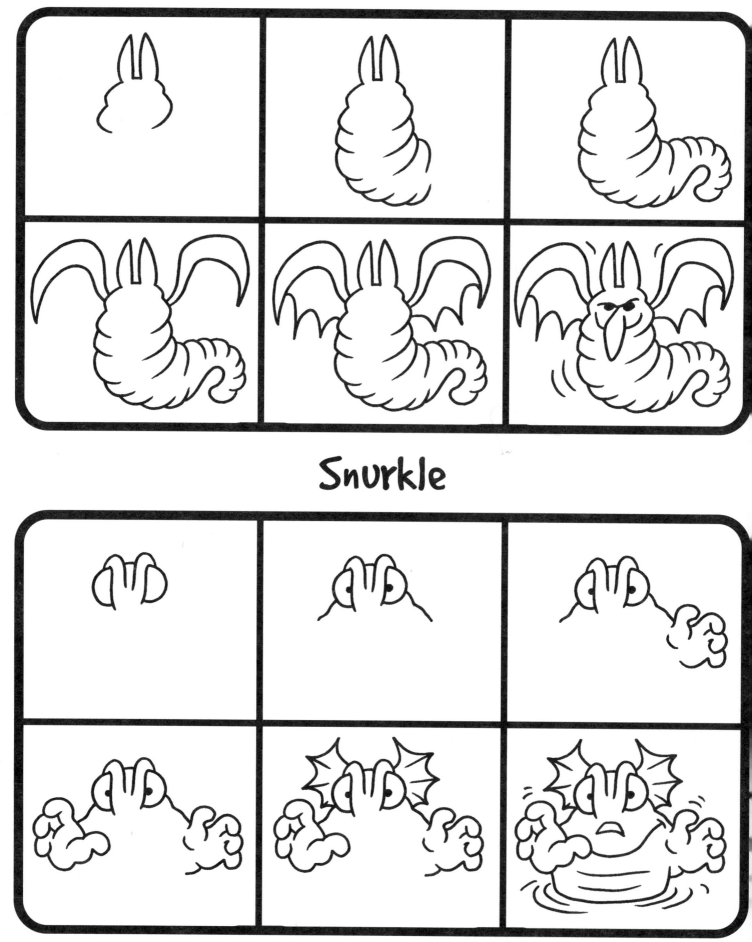

Snurkle

Mertle

Spider

Shaggy

Wavy

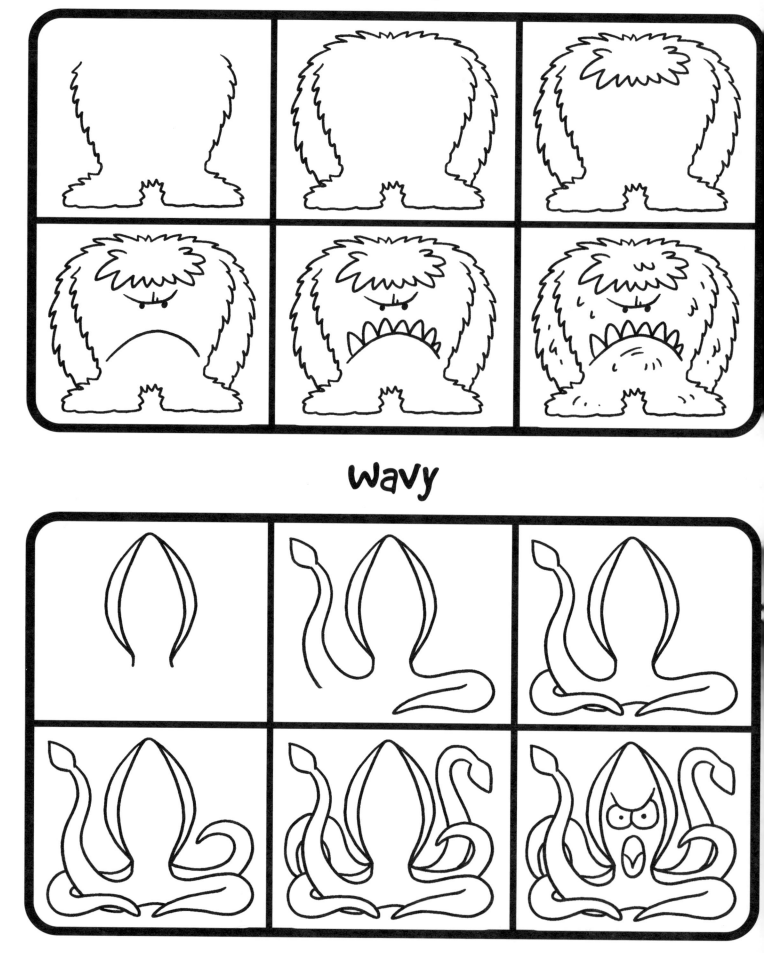

Pet

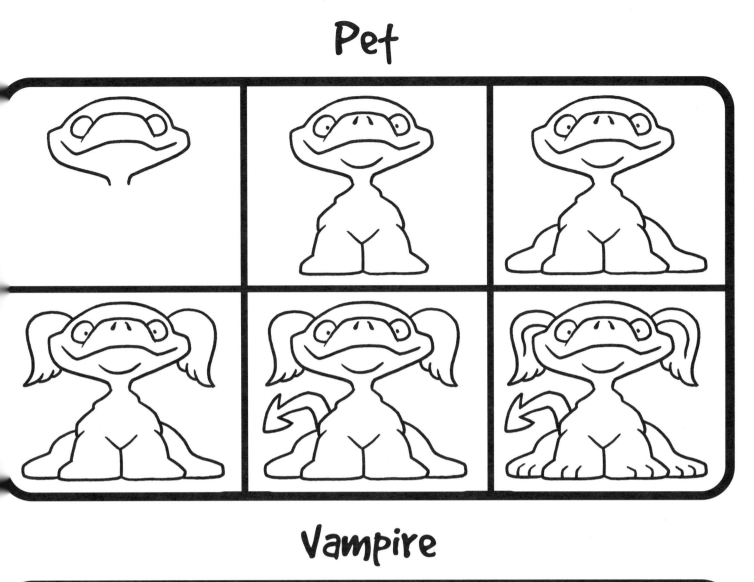

Vampire

Rah

Blob

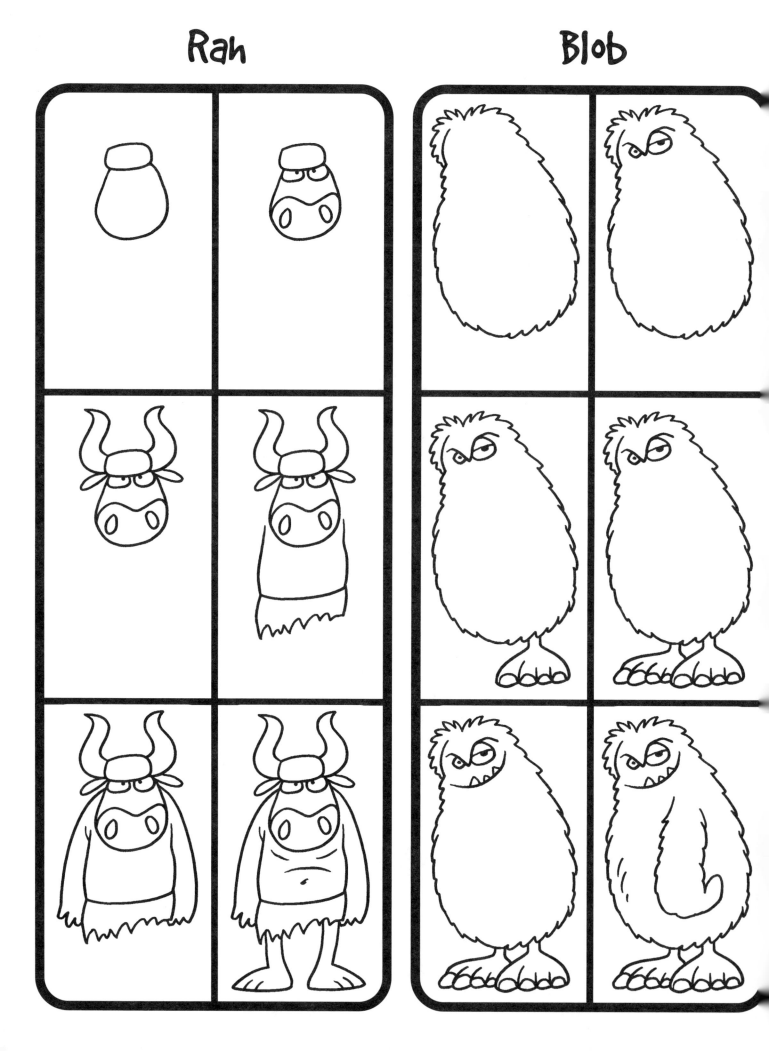

Dev   Rock

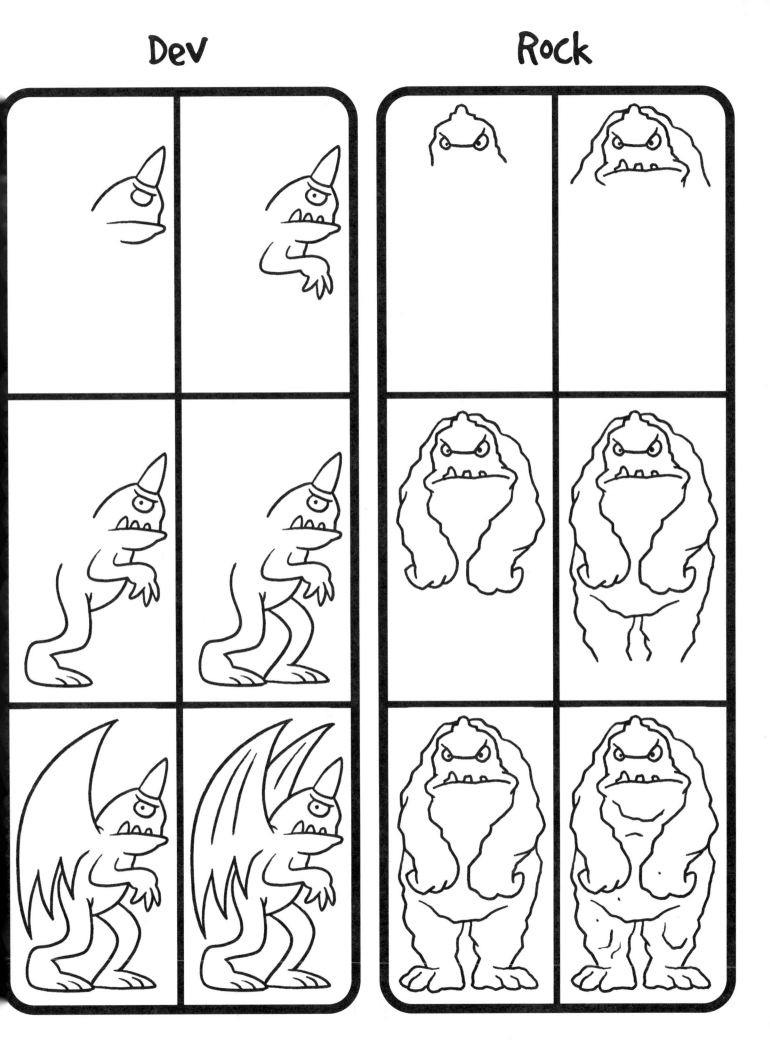

Slimey

Slug

Flokk

Gumble

Warty

Dragon

Ted

Smelly

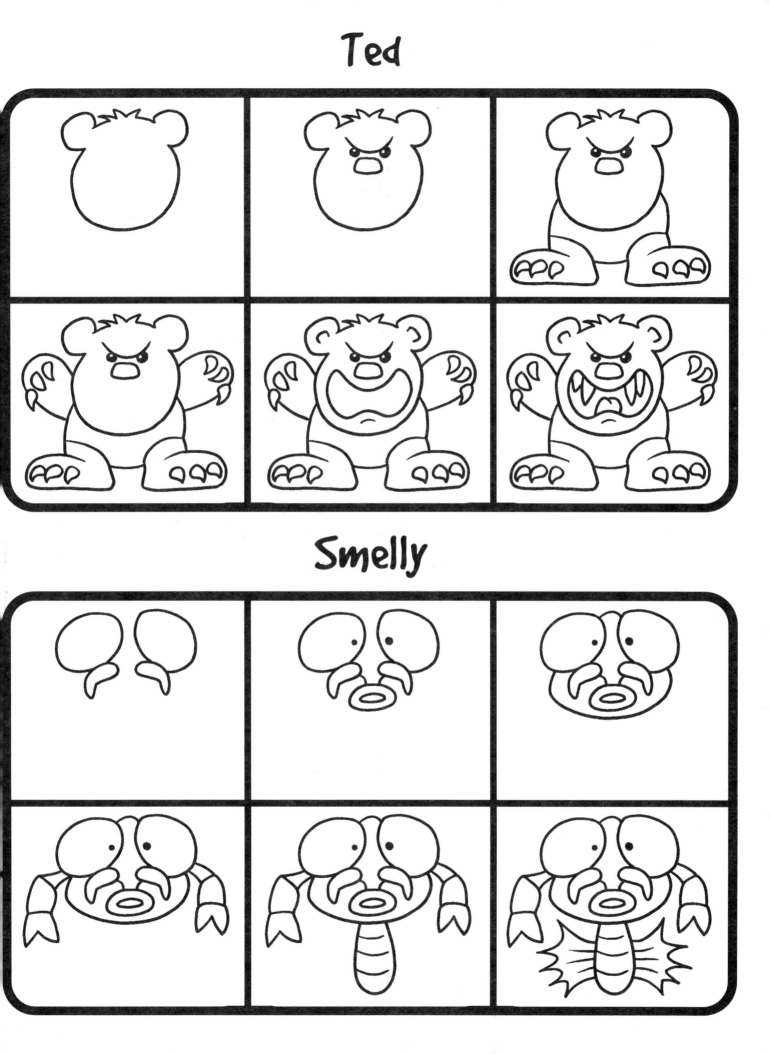

colly

cloaked

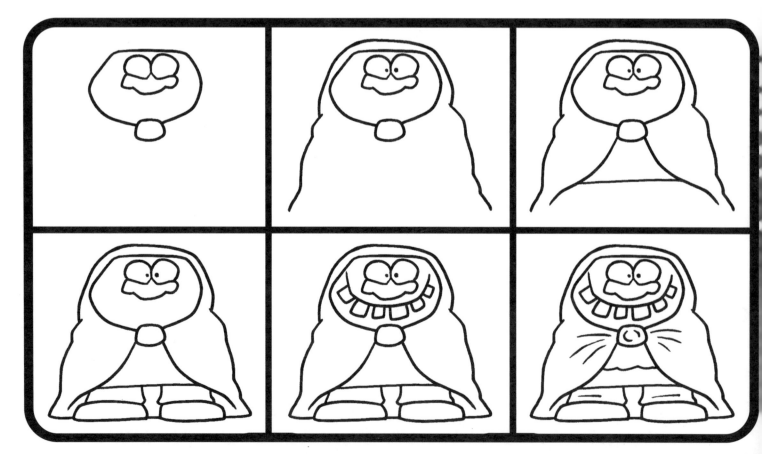

Sharky

Larry

Potty   Verm

Horn

Tree

Stocky

Mummy

Big one

Bendy

Eavesdrop

Squabble

Skull

Snail

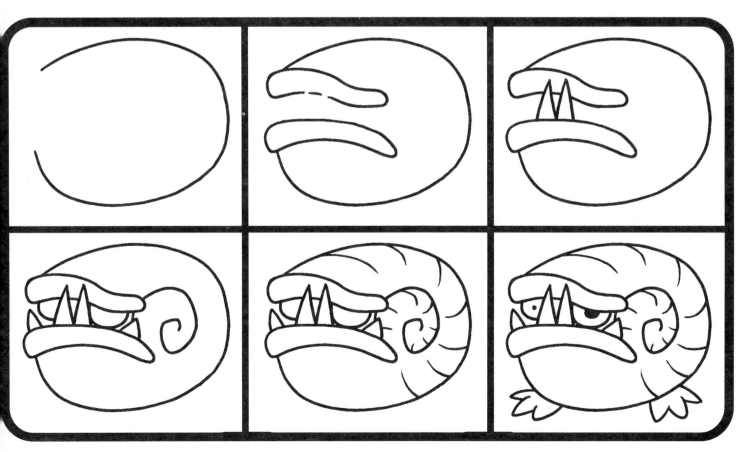

Rambo

Gloom

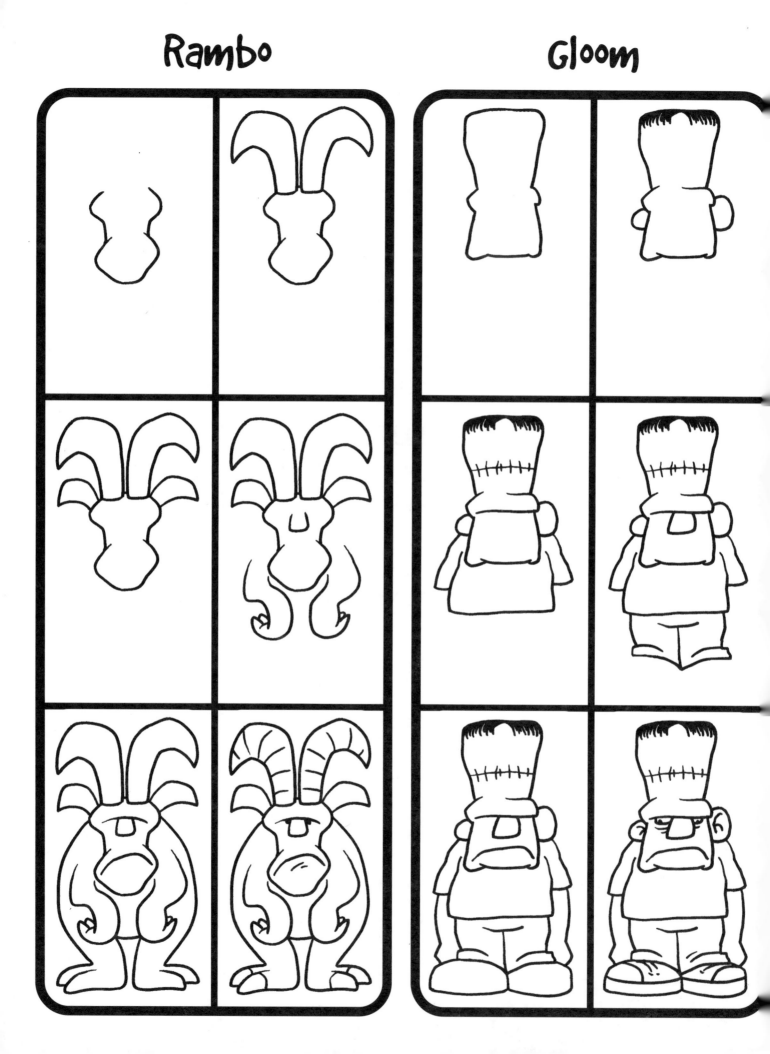

cyclops   Glum

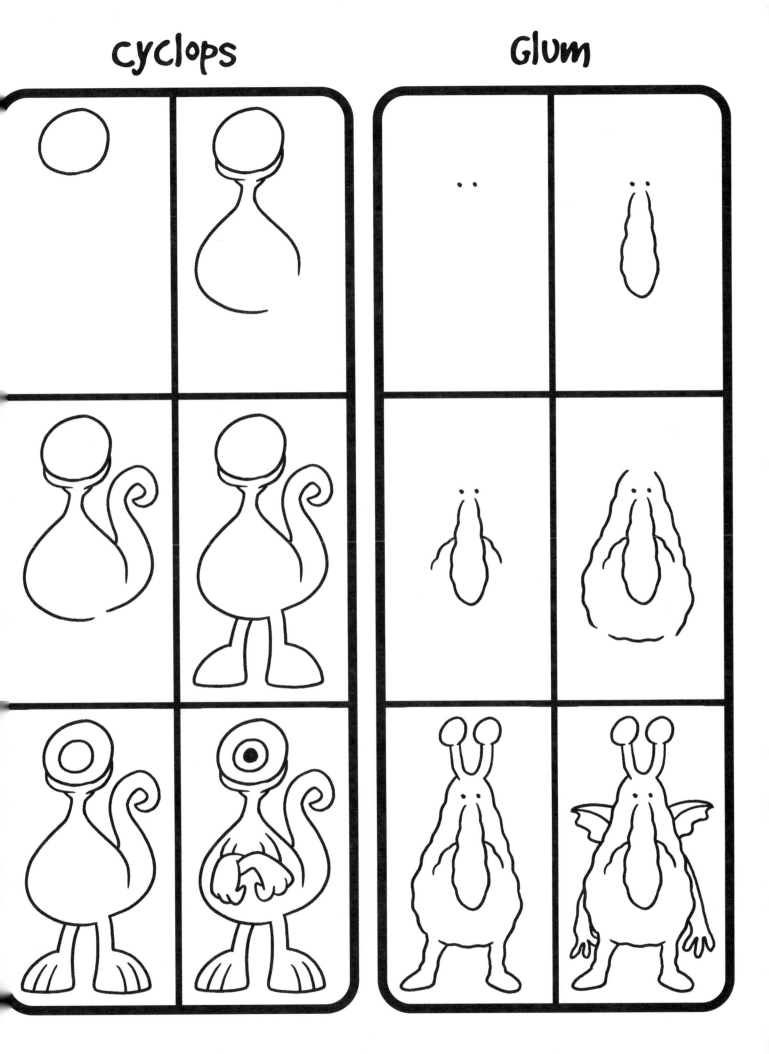

Scary

Medusa

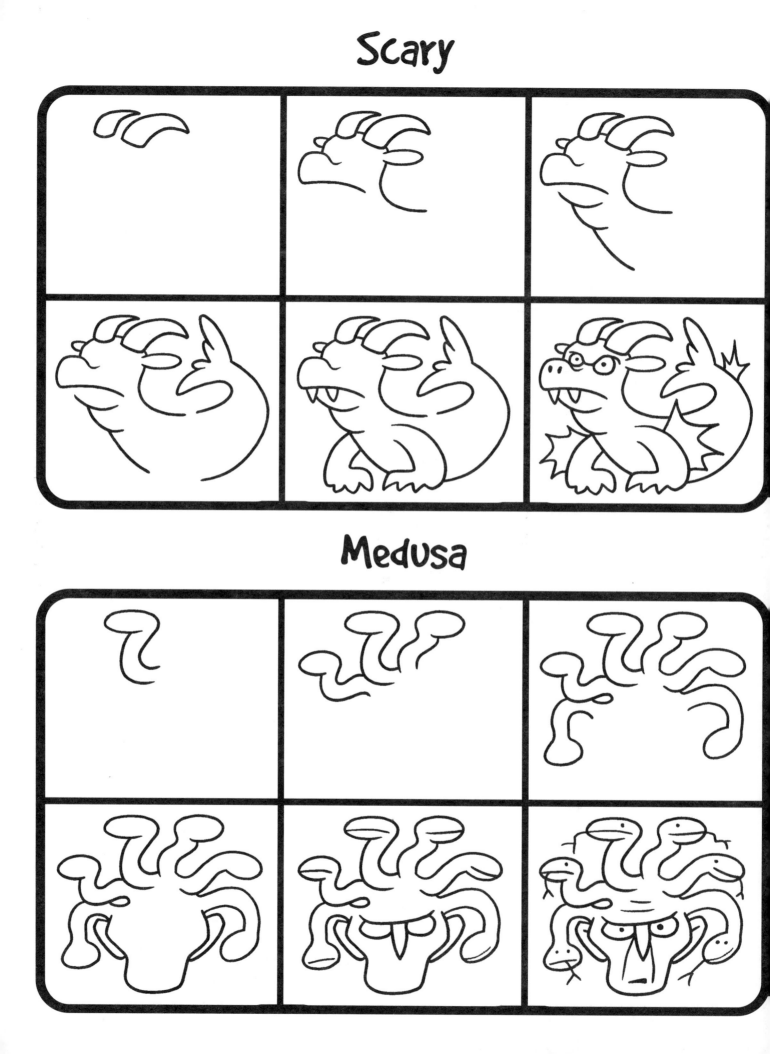

Jagged

Aaargh!

Troll

Bert

Hal

Nerd

Phantom

Squat

Werewolf

Robot

Lippy

Merlin

Granny   # Grandad

fingers

Pumpkin

Spot

Triton

Baby

Happy

Growl

Wingding

Google

Johnny

Exterminate

Vanilla

Hattie

Bulldog

Venus flytrap

Slurp

Horned Beast

Big Mouth

Snorkel

Helmet

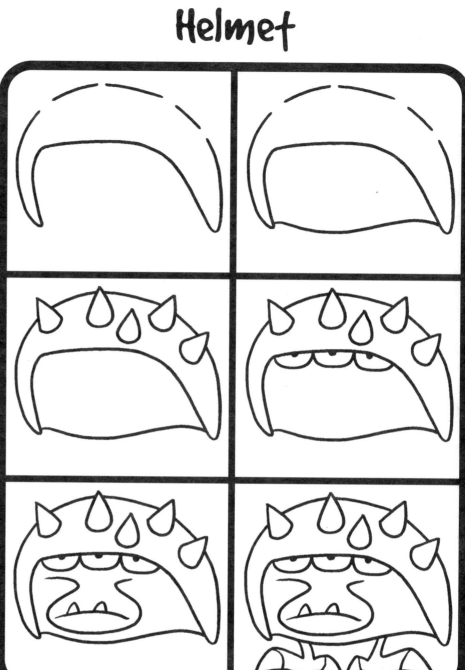

Herm

Beaky

Woo

Slump

Goggle Eyes

Truck

Slime